Dedicated to
Cameron, Elizabeth and Isabel;
the inspiration for everything

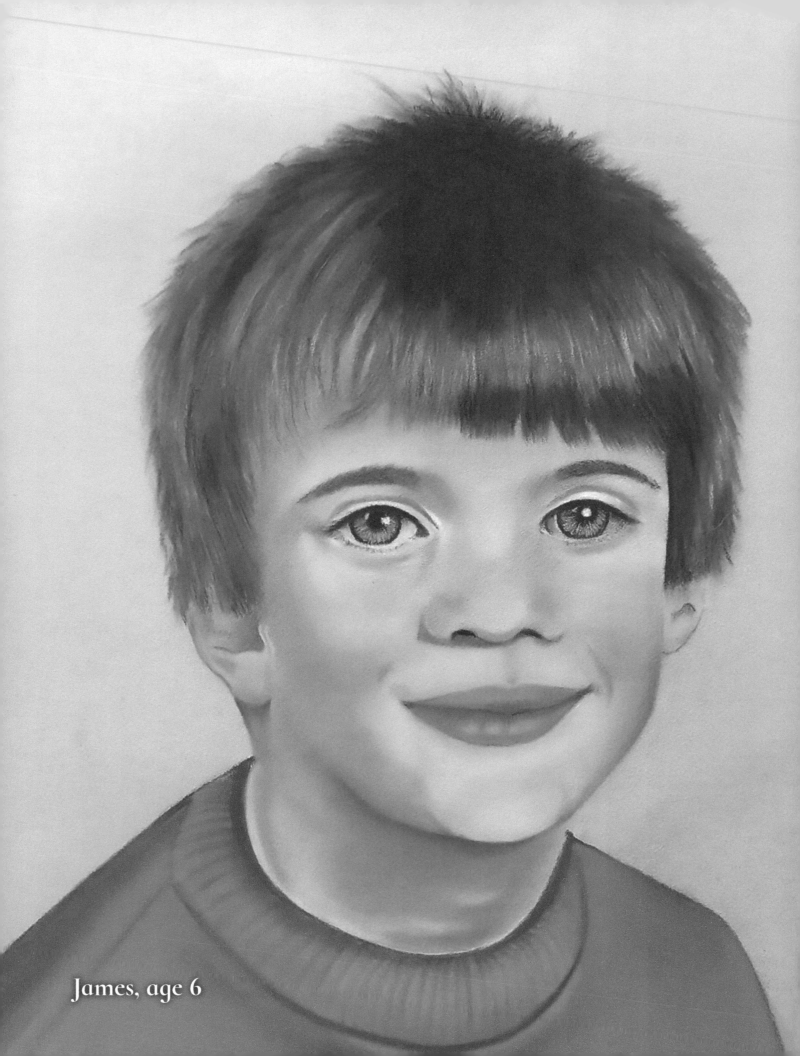

James, age 6

The Climb

Written by: Martin Bissett

Illustrated by: Pamela Carter

Illustrations by: Pamela Carter
Book design & Publishing Management by: SWATT Books Ltd

Printed in the United Kingdom
First Printing, 2022

ISBN: 978-1-7397421-0-2 (Paperback)

 Upward Spiral Press
Rossendale, England

Time is like a dream

In dreams, you can start a day before it has started in real life.

Some days look like
other days.

Some days are
incredible.

And some days arrive that you've been
waiting all your days to arrive.

On THIS day James had finally earned the money...

...he needed for a toy his heart was set on.

He even washed the
dishes for his mum.

It was worth it because of
the climb that lay ahead.

After his tasks were completed, he ran to his grandma's cabinet where his dad had put his pocket money that he had earned.

Today was THE day.

His final coin had given him the exact amount of money, to the penny, that he needed to buy his toy.

James stood at the foot of a big steep, green hill.
At the top of the hill stood a shop or shack.

In the window of the shop was a
toy James had set his heart on.
Nothing was more important to
him, than to purchase the toy.

And so began the climb...

James struggled greatly with the difficulty of the climb and the incline of the hill. The thinness of the air and the force of the wind pressed back down against him, as if it was trying to stop him from what he had set out to achieve.

Sometimes the force of the wind was so strong, he could hardly walk.

After hours and hours of climbing, that seemed to stretch throughout the whole day, James could finally see the shop on the crest of the hill.

His heart rate increased as he gave his last burst of energy to reach the shop.

As the shop drew within a few feet of him, he could see the toy.

It looked even more
magnificent and desirable
than he had imagined.

He looked deep into the shop.

And there it was. The toy he
had worked so hard for.

As he approached the front step of the door to
the shop, he suddenly noticed a man to his left,
sat slumped against the wall of the shop.

His appearance was dishevelled, his face unshaven,
his body unwashed, his clothing unwearable and his
feet were bare but his eyes were a deep Baltic blue, the
like of which James had never encountered before.

Without saying a word, he directed his gaze at James and held out one cupped hand.

James knew that he had come all this way
for the toy and that if he even gave the man
one penny from his piggy bank, he would
not have enough left for the toy which
his heart was so steadfastly set on.

James looked at the man then at the toy, then back to him, then back towards the toy; over and over again.

Finally, James paused, silence overpowered him. James looked at the toy one last time, James looked at the man, one last time...

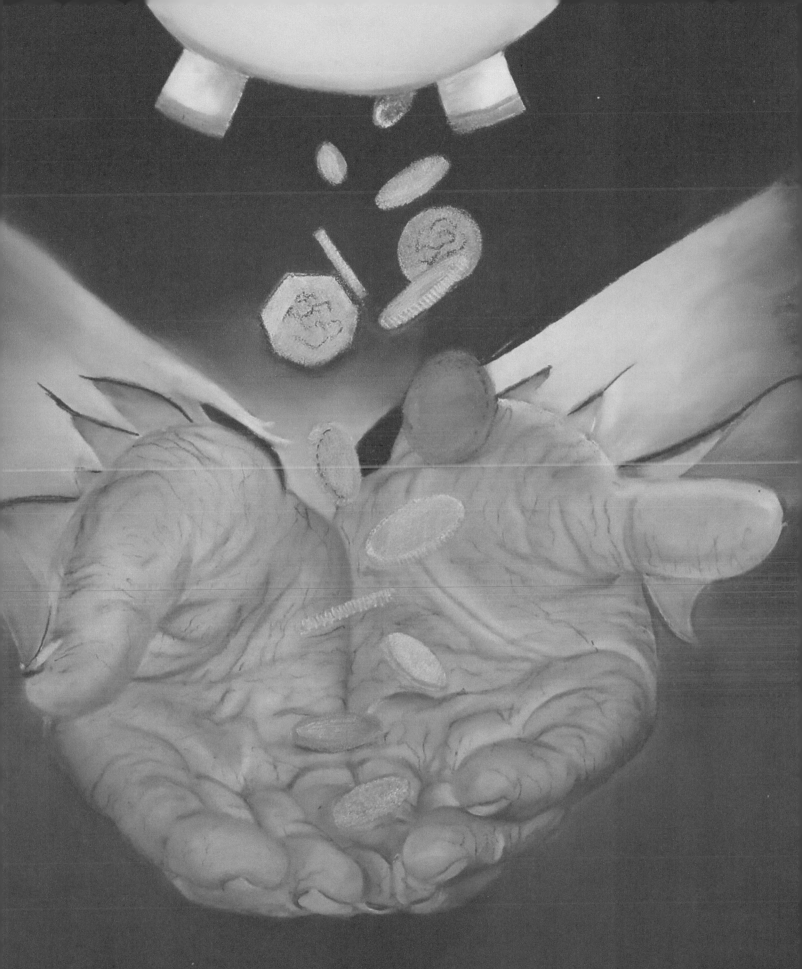

James decided to give him ALL the coins in his piggy bank.

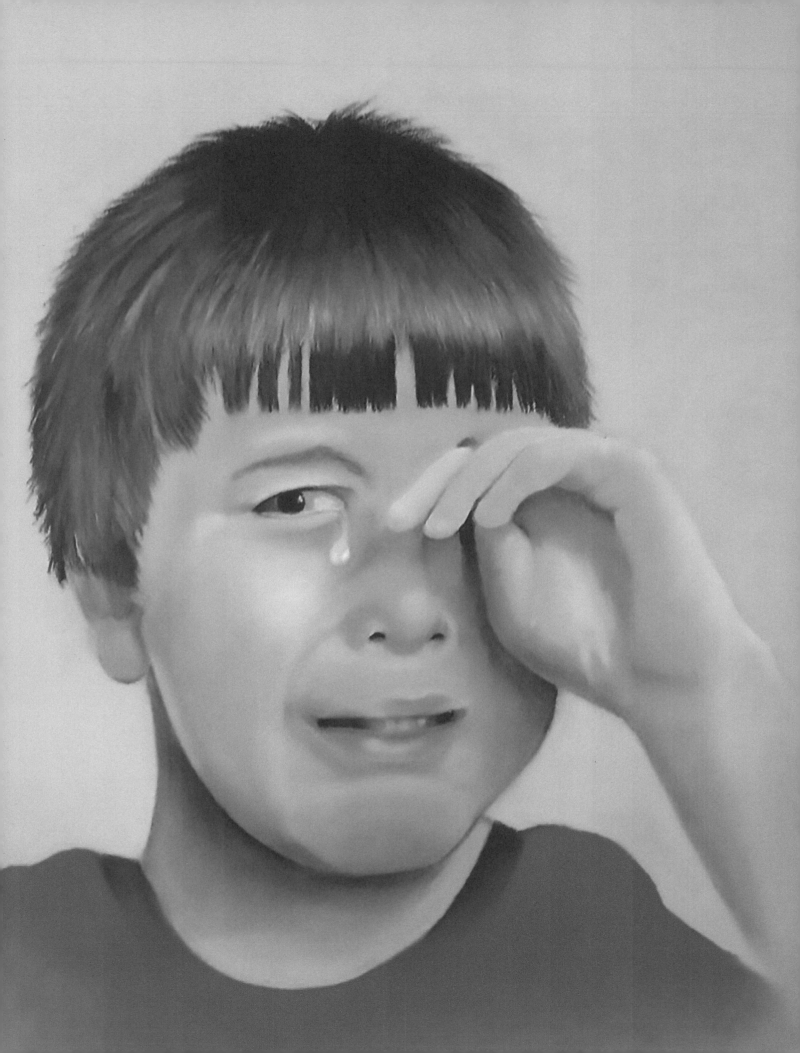

James set off back down the hill, crying his eyes out.

But James had learned who he was at his core, what he stood for and what was most important to him.

I know these things too.

And I know this because of a dream
I had when I was six years old.

About the Author

Martin Bissett, aged 6

About the Illustrator

Pamela Carter

Pam too had a dream, which was to pursue a career in paediatric physiotherapy.

When a back injury put paid to that, she retrained as a teacher of adults. A mini stroke struck in 2013 and Pam decided to go on a cruise as part of her recuperation. On the ship she joined an art class and the rest is history.

Since then Pam has delivered many commissions as she has refined her style in watercolour and pastels.

All profit from this book goes to support
The Upward Spiral Foundation,
whose purpose is to help people to feel less helpless, hopeless and homeless

Want to be a star in someone else's life? Scan the QR Code to purchase
a 'The Climb' art print, mug or many other items in the shop.